BATMAN

IS TRUSTWORTHY

Written by
CHRISTOPHER HARBO

Illustrated by
OTIS FRAMPTON

BATMAN created by
Bob Kane with
Bill Finger

Capstone Young Readers
a capstone imprint

Batman is trustworthy. He is honest and truthful. The people of Gotham City can depend on him to do the right thing.

When Commissioner Gordon lights the Bat-Signal, the Dark Knight always answers the call.

Gordon trusts Batman to help him fight crime.

When a puzzle stumps the Gotham City police,
Batman always accepts the challenge.

The police trust Batman to help them solve the riddle.

When criminals clown around in a grocery store, Batman always helps tidy up.

The grocer trusts the Dark Knight with cleanup in a sticky aisle 9.

Before the Dynamic Duo goes on patrol, Batman carefully tests the Boy Wonder's gear.

Robin trusts the Dark Knight to help keep him safe.

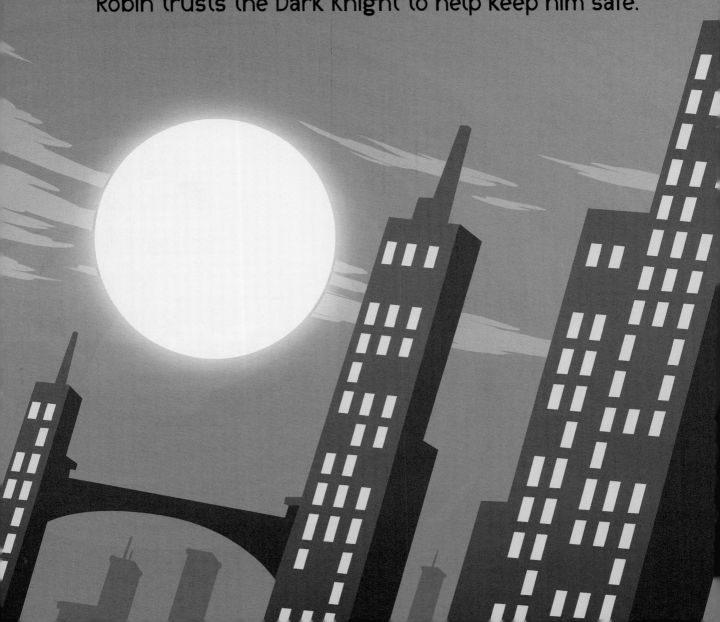

When a friend is in trouble, the Caped Crusader quickly lends a hand.

Batgirl trusts Batman to set her free.

If an accident happens in the Batcave, Batman isn't afraid to admit his mistake.

Alfred trusts Batman to always tell the truth.

When a cat burglar strikes a jewelry store, Batman tracks down the loot.

The store owner trusts Batman to return the stolen jewels.

When the fate of others rests on the flip of a coin,
Batman boldly takes action.

The people of Gotham City trust Batman to protect them.

Whenever the villains of Gotham City cause trouble, Batman bravely joins the fight.

Like it or not . . . they can trust Batman to bring them to justice!

BATMAN SAYS...

- Being trustworthy means people can rely on you for help, like when Commissioner Gordon relies on me to protect Gotham City.

- Being trustworthy means you are a loyal friend, like when I help Batgirl out of a jam.

- Being trustworthy means you are always honest, like when I admit my mistakes to my butler, Alfred.

- Being trustworthy means having the courage to do the right thing, like when I stand up to super-villains.

- Being trustworthy means being the very best you that you can be!

BE YOUR BEST
with the World's Greatest Super Heroes!

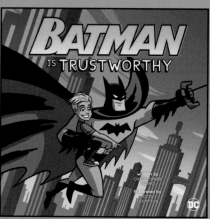

ONLY FROM CAPSTONE!

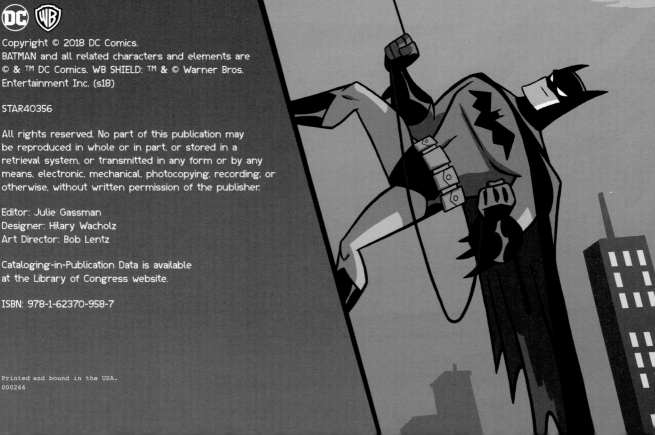

DC Super Heroes Character Education
is published by Capstone Young Readers
A Capstone Imprint
1710 Roe Crest Drive
North Mankato, Minnesota 56003
www.mycapstone.com

STAR40356

Editor: Julie Gassman
Designer: Hilary Wacholz
Art Director: Bob Lentz

Cataloging-in-Publication Data is available
at the Library of Congress website.

ISBN: 978-1-62370-958-7

Printed and bound in the USA.
000266

BATMAN

IS TRUSTWORTHY

written by
CHRISTO...
HARB...

illustrated by
OTIS
FRAMPTON